written by **SANDRA GILBERT BRÜG**

Illustrated by **ELISABETH MOSENG**

SOCCER Beat

MARGARET K. McELDERRY BOOKS

New York • London • Toronto • Sydney • Singapore

Soccer players' nimble feet

hustle at the soccer meet—

Kick it   move it
                zig-
                    zag
                        s l i d e

Dressed in cleats
they spin
and
g l i d e

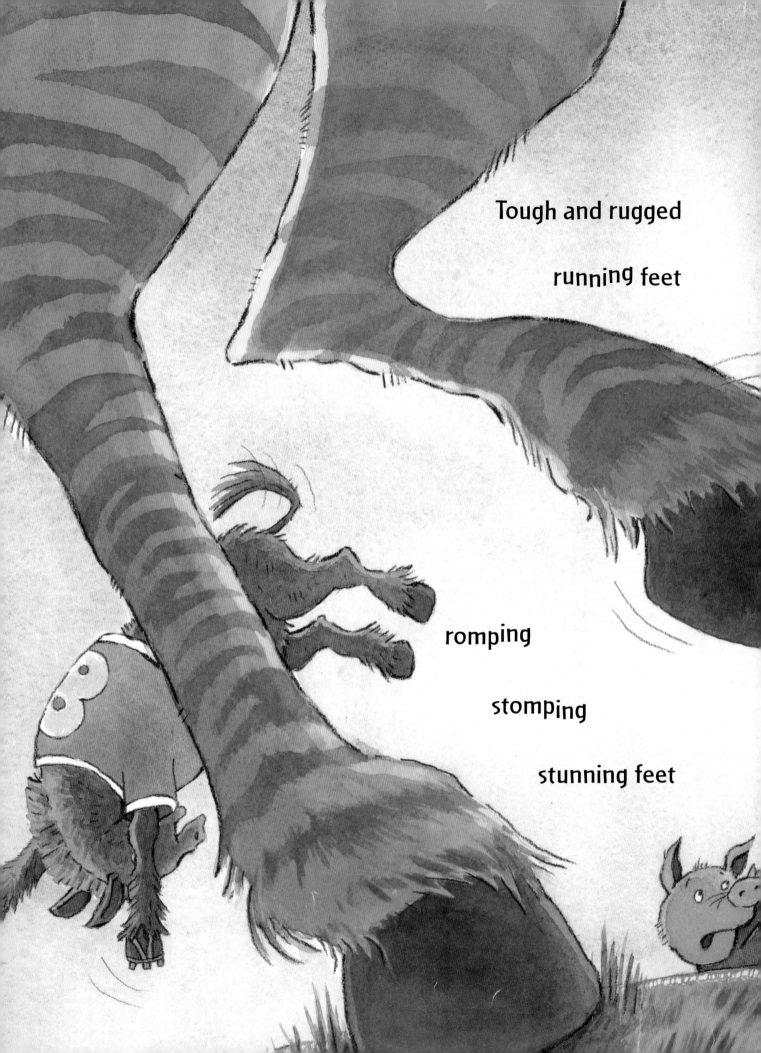

Tough and rugged

running feet

romping

stomping

stunning feet

Slapping tapping twirling feet
boogie-woogie whirling feet

On the green two teams are prancing

Rockets leaping

Cheetahs chancing

Sleek—
the Cheetahs' paws
are pouncing

tripping   rolling

sneaking   bouncing

Bold—
the spunky Rockets jumping

shin guards clashing

hard heads thumping

Cheetahs seize the ball and charge

sprinting

guarding

looming large

bodies bashing   feet the other way are dashing

On the side   the coaches barking

stamping pacing   praising sparking

Frantic fans on tippy-toe

wave their banners—GO TEAM GO!

send it flying   down the field   the goalie's spying

In the cage   his gaze is steady

crouching   wary   always ready

Skip it   hop it

pass it   pop it–

toward the net—

Oh, who can stop it?

Dribble
  dribble
    faster   more!   SLAM that checkered ball—

to SCORE!

The Cheetahs		The Rockets	
1	Three-toed Sloth	1	Wild Boar
2	Bulldog	2	Dromedary
3	Zebra	3	Sheep
4	Ostrich	4	Penguin
5	Giraffe	5	Goat
6	Pig	6	Hen
7	Beaver	7	Giant Turtle
8	Cheetah	8	Ass
9	Kangaroo	9	Eurasian Badger
10	Giant Anteater	10	Malayan Tapir
11	Striped Skunk	11	Goose

To Emma Dryden and Lee Bennett Hopkins,
with my heartfelt thanks
—S. G. B.

For Dynamite Hannah
—E. M.

Margaret K. McElderry Books
An imprint of Simon & Schuster Children's Publishing Division
1230 Avenue of the Americas, New York, New York 10020
Text copyright © 2003 by Sandra Gilbert Brüg
Illustrations copyright © 2003 by Elisabeth Moseng
All rights reserved, including the right of reproduction in whole or in part in any form.
Book design by Kristin Smith
The text for this book is set in Cafeteria.
The illustrations for this book are rendered in watercolor.
Manufactured in China
10 9 8 7 6 5 4 3 2 1
Library of Congress Cataloging-in-Publication Data
Brüg, Sandra Gilbert.
Soccer beat / Sandra Gilbert Brüg ; illustrated by Elisabeth Moseng.
p. cm.
Summary: Illustrations and rhyming text describe the action of an animal soccer game.
ISBN 0-689-84580-4
[1. Animals—Fiction. 2. Soccer—Fiction. 3. Stories in rhyme.] I. Moseng, Elisabeth, ill. II. Title.
PZ8.3.B8255 So 2003
[E]—dc21
2002002403

FIRST
EDITION